PRAISE FOR THE

Miranda AND MAUDE

SERIES

An Amazon Best Book of the Month

"Brilliantly relevant, playful, and compassionate."
—Abby Hanlon, author of *Dory Fantasmagory*

"This unlikely combination of royalty and social justice delivers fun, learning, and laughs."
—*Kirkus Reviews*

"A totally delightful story guaranteed to please young readers." —*School Library Journal*

Amulet Books
New York

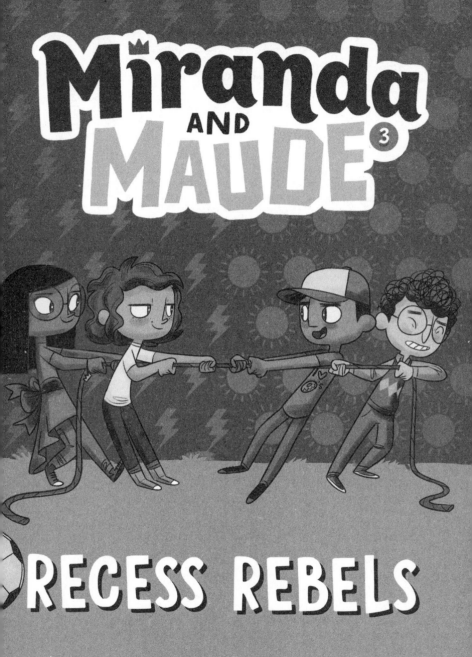

Miranda AND MAUDE³

RECESS REBELS

BY EMMA WUNSCH ✏ ILLUSTRATED BY JESSIKA VON INNEREBNER

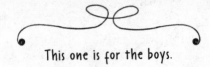

This one is for the boys.

And the girls, too.

Cataloging-in-Publication Data has been applied for and may be obtained from the Library of Congress.

Paperback ISBN 978-1-4197-4088-6

Text copyright © 2019 Emma Wunsch
Illustrations copyright © 2019 Jessika von Innerebner
Book design by Siobhán Gallagher

Printed and bound in U.S.A.
10 9 8 7 6 5 4 3 2 1

Amulet Books are available at special discounts when purchased in quantity for premiums and promotions as well as fundraising or educational use. Special editions can also be created to specification. For details, contact specialsales@abramsbooks.com or the address below.

Amulet Books® is a registered trademark of Harry N. Abrams, Inc.

ABRAMS The Art of Books
195 Broadway, New York, NY 10007
abramsbooks.com

THE

Miranda AND MAUDE

SERIES

Book One: *The Princess and the Absolutely Not a Princess*

Book Two: *Banana Pants!*

Book Three: *Recess Rebels*

WITHOUT SWINGS, SCHOOL WOULD BE ABSOLUTELY DREADFUL

Not long ago, during recess at Mountain River Valley Elementary, a princess named Miranda Rose Lapointsetta and an absolutely not a princess named Maude Brandywine Mayhew Kaye were swinging.

"Swinging is the best part of school," Maude hollered as they soared through the air. "Without swings, school would be absolutely dreadful."

Maude was shouting so Miranda could hear her. Although they tried to swing at the exact same time, the laws of motion made that impossible. Sometimes Maude's words flew over Miranda's ears. Other times Miranda's words flew under Maude's head.

Miranda nodded, pretty sure she'd understood. Swinging with Maude was definitely the best part of the day. Of course, there were other things at school the girls liked, most especially their teacher, Miss Kinde. Miss Kinde was so amazingly wonderful that, not long ago, for two whole weeks, she'd let their class (3B) put on a play called *Banana Pants* instead of taking tests!

The play hadn't been perfect. Costumes had ripped, lines were mumbled, and one dance routine was completely forgotten. But the class had come together and worked extremely hard, which Miss Kinde had said made it a successful creative endeavor and, most importantly, a wonderful experience.

Unfortunately, now that the curtain had closed on *Banana Pants*, 3B was back to taking a preposterous number of Mandatory National Reading and Writing and Math Exam practice exams, because Mountain River Valley Elementary School's principal, Principal Fish, thought they were *extremely* important.

Neither Maude nor Miranda liked practice exams. Other things they didn't like: music class, PE, and school lunches. Also, the girls thought that the school day was very long, there were too many rules, and they had to be quiet a lot.

Actually, Miranda didn't mind being quiet. A lot of the time she was a quiet person.

Maude was not quiet. She was often loud with lots to say.

Right now, she was saying, "I just don't get tag." She pointed at the playground, where kids from their class were running around screaming, "Not It!"

Miranda, who was afraid of heights, looked down quickly. She watched Donut leap past

Norbert, who sprinted past Fletcher, who jogged away from Felix. Miranda didn't think this looked fun because she didn't like running or screaming. But Felix and Donut were grinning. It was hard to tell how Norbert and Fletcher felt because they were moving so fast.

Miranda looked back up at Maude. "Some people find it fun, I guess. Just like we like swinging."

"I guess." Maude shrugged and pointed down to Hillary Greenlight-Miller, who was, as usual, walking across the balance beam. "There's Hillary—balancing, of course."

Miranda quickly admired Hillary's excellent balance.

"What are they doing?" Maude pointed to a grassy spot in the middle of the playground where their classmates Agnes, Agatha, and Desdemona were lying on their backs holding soccer balls in the air.

"Probably playing one of Desdemona's animal games," Miranda said.

At that moment, Donut, who was still trying to avoid getting tagged, ran past the girls.

Desdemona jumped up. "Girl tag!" she shouted.

Donut turned around but kept jogging. "No," he hollered. "No girl tag! Girl tag is forbidden!"

Maude slowed her swing. "What did Donut say?" She looked at Miranda.

Miranda gulped. Maude's question sounded a lot like the ones on the morning practice exam: tricky and without a clear answer.

"I think Donut just forbade Desdemona from playing tag because she's a girl!" Maude screeched. "We might be soaring thousands of feet in the air, but I have excellent hearing, and my ears are super-duper clean because I took a bath last night and a shower this morning because I forgot about my bath until I was in the shower."

"The playground is so loud. I'm not sure I heard what Donut said," Miranda said quietly.

"I am," Maude said. And without bothering to come to a complete stop (and thus breaking rule fifty-two in the *Official Rules of Mountain River Valley Elementary*), she flew off her swing and ran over to Desdemona.

2

WE CAN'T STAND FOR THIS!

"We can't stand for this!" Maude shrieked to Desdemona, Agatha, and Agnes, who were now all standing up.

"Stand for what?" Desdemona dribbled her ball toward Agatha very slowly. "We're playing sloth soccer."

"For this unjustness! Donut has forbidden you from playing tag!" Maude hollered. "Because you're a girl!"

Desdemona leisurely lifted the ball with her foot. "He did?"

"Yes! When he ran past you. Miranda heard it too." Maude looked at Miranda, who hesitated, then nodded slowly.

Desdemona shrugged. "Oh. That wasn't nice, but soccer is better. And sloth soccer is the best!" In slow motion, she kicked the ball to Agnes.

"That's not the point!" Maude said.

"What's the point?" Agatha asked. She kicked the ball slowly to Maude.

Maude climbed up on the soccer ball and promptly fell off. "Forbidding you from tag is forbidding us all from tag. The poet Maya Angelou once said, 'Each time a woman stands up for herself, she stands up for all women.' I stand here now on behalf of all Three B girls to officially declare that we won't tolerate not being allowed to play tag!"

What a good speech, Miranda thought. Then she had another thought. "Do you want to play tag, Maude?"

Maude looked curiously at Miranda. "Not

at all," she said. "But that's not the point! The point is that we *should* be able to play tag if we want to."

The girls nodded. They could certainly do everything the boys did.

But unfortunately, what they needed to do right now was line up, since the bell ending recess had just rung. The soccer girls kicked their balls toward the goal. The boys, still playing tag, ran over to 3B's line. Maude ran back to the swings to grab her messenger bag, which she'd brought outside even though it broke rule seventy-four.

Once in line, Maude bent down to secure the leftover half of her delicious but super-stinky Limburger cheese sandwich, which was in danger of falling out of her bag. Unfortunately, at that same moment, Donut, who was frantically trying to not get tagged by Fletcher, spun around and crashed into her. Maude fell forward and knocked into Hillary Greenlight-Miller, who bumped into Miranda.

"You're It!" Fletcher sounded victorious.

"Ow!" Maude hollered.

"My leg," Hillary cried. "My leg, my leg, my leg!"

Miranda didn't say anything. She was fine and more concerned with the things that had fallen out of Maude's bag. Maude was famous (in 3B) for the strange things she brought to school. Miranda peered at the pile, very worried when she saw Maude's leftover cheese sandwich.

"I have a balance competition soon," Hillary wailed. "That's why I spend every recess on the balance beam! I can't get hurt!" She glared at Maude.

"It wasn't me," Maude shrieked. "It was him!" She pointed at Donut. "*He's* the reason we're on the ground. Are you all right, Hillary?" Hillary Greenlight-Miller liked being best or first at everything. This used to annoy Maude, but ever since Hillary had done a great job directing *Banana Pants*, it had annoyed her a little less.

Hillary slowly stood up. "Maybe."

Maude pointed to the pile next to her and scowled at Donut. "Now all my stuff is on the ground and I'm going to be late! This is all your fault!"

"Oh," Donut said. "Sorry. I didn't see you. And you're not supposed to have your bag at recess anyway."

"Humph," Maude said. "Tag is the worst game!"

"I'll help you, Maude," Miranda said. She gulped a mouthful of air so she wouldn't have to breathe near Maude's sandwich. Quickly, the girls stuffed Maude's things back into her bag. And then, right on time, they walked back into class.

3

DONUT'S BRILLIANT IDEA

Walking into 3B behind Maude and Miranda was Donut. Donut loved doughnuts. He also loved tag. *Maude is wrong*, Donut thought as he sat down. Tag was the best game! It was free and didn't require any equipment. Why did Maude have so much weird stuff in her bag? If she'd been standing up like she was supposed to, he would've seen her. *And* Fletcher wouldn't have tagged him. Now he'd be It until the dismissal bell rang, which felt like three hundred hours away.

Donut looked at Saeed, a new student, in the row in front of him. If Donut shifted four inches to the right, he'd just be able to reach Saeed's shoulder. He'd have to do it quickly so Miss Kinde wouldn't see. But that could be extra fun! Quietly, Donut tapped Saeed.

Saeed turned around.

"You're It," Donut whispered.

Saeed laughed, reached over, and tapped Felix.

Within twenty-seven seconds, all of the boys in 3B were happily playing secret silent inside tag.

And the girls in the class were not happy about that!

4

INSIDE TAG IS QUADRUPLE ANNOYING

Actually, just one girl noticed the inside tag.

"If it was annoying outside, then it's quadruple annoying inside," Maude told Miranda and Hillary as Miss Kinde handed out the afternoon practice exam. "And dangerous!"

Hillary nodded, rubbed her leg, and wrote her name on her exam.

Miranda wrote her name and read question one, which, like question one on the morning exam, was horribly confusing.

Maude didn't write her name or read the first question. She put on a pair of glasses that she loved but didn't need and watched Felix tag Norris, Norris tag Fletcher, Fletcher tag Norbert, Norbert tag Saeed, and Saeed tag Donut. Then she groaned loudly.

"Everyone should be working *quietly*." Miss

Kinde looked up from the mountain of morning practice exams she was grading. "Please work quietly, Maude."

What? Maude's heart fluttered, then sputtered. She had done absolutely nothing wrong. This was Donut's fault! She wasn't breaking the rules by playing inside tag. She was just trying to take another dumb practice exam. *This isn't fair*, Maude thought. First, Donut forbade girls to play tag! Then, because of tag, she was knocked to the ground! And all of her stuff was knocked over and possibly broken or lost! And now she was being yelled at! By the best teacher in the universe! Something had to be done! Maude just didn't know what!

5

MAUDE'S LONG AFTERNOON

Amazingly, the rest of the afternoon zipped by for Donut. Secret silent inside tag made school a lot of fun, even the really boring parts. Tag during the practice exam was surprisingly easy, but during music with cranky Mr. Mancini? Not easy at all! Getting away with tagging Felix at the exact moment Principal Fish walked down the hall looking for rule-breakers? Well, that was probably the greatest moment of Donut's elementary school life.

The day went by at the regular Monday-afternoon speed for most everybody else in 3B but painfully slowly for Maude, who couldn't pay attention to anything but the boys' silly game. How come none of the teachers noticed them playing? Why did Mr. Mancini tell her to stop playing her harmonica but say nothing when Fletcher tagged Donut? And why hadn't

Desdemona been mad about Donut not wanting her to play tag because she's a girl? What gave Donut the right to say who could play tag? It was such an injustice!

But just as Donut was about to tag Felix while walking back to 3B after music, Principal Fish walked by. *Hooray*, Maude thought, feeling hopeful for the first time since recess. Principal Fish would see what was happening, and Donut would finally get in trouble! Tag shouldn't be played in school! Tag shouldn't be played at all! She imagined rule 10,002 in the *Official Rules of Mountain River Valley Elementary*: tag, both inside and outside, would be totally forbidden! *Or maybe*, Maude thought, *tag, both inside and outside, would be totally forbidden FOR THE BOYS!* The girls could play if they wanted to, which of course they wouldn't, because the girls knew that tag was dumb!

"Here, here!" Maude chanted, imagining Donut being marched down the hall by Principal Fish.

"Maude," Miranda said quietly. "What are you doing?"

"Huh?" Maude was jolted out of her daydream and back to 3B, right next to Donut, who had somehow gotten away with playing tag right in front of Principal Fish!

Principal Fish, Maude wondered. What would he say if Maude told him about inside tag? *Probably nothing*, Maude thought, trudging to her desk. Principal Fish only liked following the rules, not changing them. *Principal Fish's favorite rule is most certainly "follow the rules*," Maude thought as her eyes landed on her bulging messenger bag. Her wonderful messenger bag that held some of her most precious possessions, which had been brutally flung to the ground. That was probably against the rules, wasn't it? All of a sudden, Maude had a brilliant idea.

"Miss Kinde!" Maude screeched. "Miss Kinde! I must speak to Principal Fish!"

"Principal Fish?" Miss Kinde was shocked. Actually, everyone in 3B was shocked. Maude wanting to see Principal Fish was like a fish swimming out of the water to ride a bicycle. Or something like that.

Maude nodded.

"Is there anything I can do?" Miss Kinde asked gently.

"No," Maude said. "And rule forty-seven in the *Official Rules of Mountain River Valley Elementary* says that students are allowed to speak directly to the principal if they feel one hundred percent certain that their teacher would be unable to help them."

"Are you sure I can't help you?"

Maude nodded. "One hundred and ten percent."

Miss Kinde looked a little hurt and very con-fused, but she said okay.

Grabbing her bag, Maude limped out of the room.

Once she was out of 3B, Maude broke rule nineteen by going into the bathroom without a pass. Quickly, she dug into her bag and put on a few accessories.

The Maude who left the bathroom looked very different from the one who'd left 3B. This Maude wobbled into Principal Fish's office.

"HOW CAN I HELP YOU?" Principal Fish boomed.

"I'm here about rule eighty-one," Maude said, trying to sound like she was in a tremendous amount of pain.

6

A STARTLING ANNOUNCEMENT

Not long after Maude (who was not limping or bandaged) returned to 3B, Principal Fish made the following announcement over the loudspeaker:

"ATTENTION! STUDENTS OF MOUNTAIN RIVER VALLEY ELEMENTARY!" He was so loud that even the teachers covered their ears. "AS OF RIGHT NOW, TAG AT MOUNTAIN RIVER VALLEY ELEMENTARY SCHOOL IS FORBIDDEN! STRICTLY FORBIDDEN!"

"What?!" Donut shrieked.

"TAG IS PROHIBITED BECAUSE I, PRINCIPAL FISH, HAVE BEEN REMINDED THAT TAG OFFICIALLY BREAKS RULE EIGHTY-ONE, WHICH SAYS THAT ANY GAME THAT IS POTENTIALLY HAZARDOUS TO INNOCENT BYSTANDERS IS NOT ALLOWED ON SCHOOL GROUNDS."

"What innocent bystanders?" Saeed asked. "What's hazardous about tag?"

"THANK YOU FOR YOUR ATTENTION," Principal Fish hollered. "PLEASE CONTINUE WITH YOUR REGULARLY SCHEDULED LATE-AFTERNOON PRACTICE EXAM."

"Miss Kinde!" Donut wailed. "You're not going to make Three B follow this super-dumb new rule, are you?"

"I'm so sorry," Miss Kinde said sympathetically. "But we must follow Principal Fish's rules. No matter how . . ." She didn't say anything else.

"I don't get it," Donut said. "We've been playing tag forever. Why would Principal Fish stop it now?"

No one said anything.

3B was quiet.

3B was very quiet.

Except for one faint snicker from a certain girl with a mostly hidden eye patch in her pocket.

7

WE HOLD THESE TRUTHS

When the dismissal bell finally rang at Mountain River Valley that Monday, most students left as quickly as possible. Miranda and Maude were the last to go because it had taken Maude so long to pack up all of her stuff.

"It was you, right?" Miranda asked when they were outside. "You got Principal Fish to forbid tag."

Maude grinned proudly.

"How?" Miranda asked.

Maude looked to her left. She looked to her right. She looked behind her and then down at the ground. When she was sure the coast was clear, she took the sling and eye patch out of her bag and grinned. "I simply reminded Principal Fish of rule eighty-one in the *Official Rules of Mountain River Valley Elementary.*"

"But I've seen you get way more hurt

roller-skating or sliding down a tree too fast. Donut didn't mean to hurt you. And he didn't hurt your eye or your arm."

"Principal Fish doesn't know that." Maude sounded proud.

Miranda didn't know what to say. Sure, Donut had crashed into Maude, but people bumped into people all the time. Just last night, her father, King Dad (or KD, as she called him), had crashed into Chef Blue right before a boring, fancy royal dinner. Tomato soup had drenched both the chef and the king, but both had said sorry about a million times. In the end, it hadn't been that big a deal. Except they'd had pea soup, which was nobody's favorite. And yes, Miranda understood that Maude had been annoyed when everything fell out of her bag. But it didn't seem right that Maude had pretended to be hurt just to stop a game.

But then, almost like she was reading Miranda's mind, Maude said, "I am truly hurt by Donut's words. He can't forbid Desdemona from tag! Just because I don't like tag doesn't mean I shouldn't stick up for my fellow girls. We must all stand and work together. Actions speak louder than words, and in the words of Elizabeth Cady Stanton, 'We hold these truths to be self-evident, that all men and women are created equal.'"

This also made sense. Unlike Miranda, Maude knew all about rights and standing up for oneself. Was Maude right to wrap a sling on her arm and put a patch on her eye? Maude was her best friend, after all. Was this just the Maude way of doing the right thing? By the time Miranda got back to the castle, not only did she feel that particular Monday-afternoon exhaustion, she also felt extremely confused.

8

THE BOY IN THE TREE

It was true that before Maude showed Miranda her injury props, she had looked to her right, to her left, behind her, and down at the ground. But she hadn't looked up. If she had, she would've seen Donut breaking rule eleven, sitting up in the big tree in front of school.

Donut was in the tree because he was no longer allowed to play tag. Tree climbing wasn't his favorite after-school activity, but he had nothing else to do but sit there, feeling mad.

He was too high up to hear what Maude was saying, but once he saw her grinning and showing Miranda the eye patch and sling, he knew exactly why Principal Fish had decided to suddenly enforce rule eighty-one!

9

THE FIRST BOYS-ONLY MEETING

Without tag, the Mountain River Valley playground was strangely quiet Tuesday morning. Miranda and Maude were swinging, Hillary was balancing, and the rest of the girls were playing seal soccer, but the 3B boys just stood there until Donut arrived, wheeling a small suitcase.

"Meeting," he said to the group of boys. "Boys only. At the sandbox."

"The sandbox?" Saeed said. "That's where the littlest of the littlest kids go."

"I don't want the girls to hear us," Donut said.

The boys shuffled over to the sandbox, where, as Saeed had said, the littlest of the littlest kids were happily playing. Once the littlest children saw the serious 3B boys, they fled.

"I have called this boys-only meeting," Donut said quietly, "because we need to get back at the girls. The girls are the reason we're not playing tag right now."

"The girls?" Fletcher asked. "But Principal Fish made the announcement."

Donut nodded. "But the girls made it happen. Well, one did at least." Then he explained how he'd seen Maude with her eye patch and sling after school. And although he could only see the back of Miranda from his perch, he was pretty sure that she had been nodding and laughing, so she was probably most definitely in on it too.

"It's not fair," Fletcher said. "Tag is the best part of school."

"I know," Donut said. "Maude is a faker. But don't worry. I can fake better!" He opened the suitcase. "I knew there was a reason why my mom was a nurse!"

ANOTHER MEETING WITH PRINCIPAL FISH

After he finished his Tuesday-morning practice exam, Donut told Miss Kinde that he needed to talk to Principal Fish.

"Principal Fish?" Miss Kinde was shocked. No one else was shocked, though, because the rest of the class had already gone to art.

"Yes," Donut said.

"Is there anything I can do?" Miss Kinde asked.

"No," Donut said. "And rule forty-seven says students are allowed to speak directly to the principal if they feel one hundred percent certain that their teacher would be unable to help them."

"You're sure?"

Donut nodded. "One hundred and twenty percent."

Miss Kinde looked a little confused and hurt, but she said okay.

Donut wheeled his suitcase into the bathroom. Unlike Maude, he didn't break rule nineteen. He'd remembered to ask for the bathroom pass.

BY ORDER OF PRINCIPAL
FERDINAND F. FISH

Tuesday morning flew by for Maude. Not only did Mr. Van Der Zee praise her fruit still life in front of the whole class, but now that the boys were no longer playing inside tag, she'd finished her practice exam without distraction and in record time and was able to spend the rest of the period reading her new book: *Training Your Chicken in Three Easy Steps* by Patrice P. Poulet. And, to make a great morning even better, her dad had packed her another extraordinarily delicious Limburger cheese sandwich.

After lunch, as usual, 3B went out for recess.

"What should we do today?" Desdemona asked. "Sloth soccer? Monkey marbles?"

"Let's play regular soccer today," Agnes said. "I'm tired of kicking so slowly."

"Actually, now that it's not allowed, I wanna play tag," Agatha said.

"I'll be on my bal—what?" Hillary's voice cracked. "Where's my balance beam?"

"Oh, Hillary. You're so funny. Ha ha," Maude said without looking up. Even though it broke rule eighty-three, she was reading her chicken-training book while walking across the playground.

"It's gone," Hillary croaked. "My beautiful beloved beam."

"Wow," Miranda said. "It *is* gone!"

Maude put her book down. "That's bananas. Who would take your beam?"

"We would," said three exceptionally tall men with long beards wearing fancy suits, sunglasses, hard hats, and tool belts.

The girls looked up, way up, at the tall men.

"We removed the balance beam before lunch," the shortest of the tall men said.

"My beam!" Hillary wailed.

"Why?" Maude asked. "Personally, I find

balancing tremendously boring, but Hillary's competition is soon."

"We were instructed to remove the balance beam," the second-shortest tall man said. "By order of Principal Ferdinand F. Fish."

"By order of Principal Fish?" Maude asked.

"And now we will remove the swings," the tallest of the tall men said.

Maude opened her mouth but said nothing.

"Why?" Miranda asked.

The men didn't answer, since she'd spoken quietly.

"Why are you taking the swings?" Miranda asked louder. "What were Principal Fish's orders?"

"There was a report of multiple injuries," the shortest of the tall men said as he hoisted up the left side of the swing set.

The girls looked at one another. Then they looked over at the sandbox.

"The boys," Maude croaked.

"How could they do such a thing?" Hillary moaned.

"Rule eighty-one," Miranda said sadly.

"Correct!" the men said as they hoisted the right side of the swing set over their shoulders and began walking across the playground.

"Stop! This isn't fair," Maude hollered. "This injustice will not be tolerated!"

The three tall men kept walking.

Desdemona, Agnes, and Agatha clutched their soccer balls.

"Now what?" Hillary asked.

Maude closed her eyes and imagined all the brave women who had come before her. Perhaps some of those courageous women had also stood on playgrounds trying to figure out what to do when their swings were taken away. "Follow me, recess rebels," Maude commanded.

The girls followed Maude across the much emptier playground and over to the sandbox.

"How dare you have Principal Fish's gigantic men remove our swings!" Maude shouted at Donut.

"And balance beam," Hillary squawked.

"But you stopped tag," Donut said.

That's right, Miranda thought. Maude had stopped tag, so the boys had stopped balancing and swinging. Now Maude could go explain to Principal Fish that she'd made a mistake, and the boys would do the same thing, and everything could go back to normal. Miranda was about to say all this, but Maude had climbed on top of a rusty metal lunch box that was lying around and was shaking her fist.

"Tag is stupid!" Maude shouted. "So so so stupid!"

"Tag is *not* stupid!" Donut hollered. "Balance beams are stupid! And swings are the stupidest thing of all. This dumb rope is better than the stupid old swings!" He picked up a long yellow rope that was on the ground.

"Hey! That's my rope," Maude said. "It must have fallen out of my bag when you pushed me!"

"He didn't push you," Miranda said quietly. "He just bumped into you."

"Don't call my rope dumb!" Maude yelled. "It has zillions of purposes!"

"Like what?" Donut asked.

Maude was so angry she couldn't think of a single purpose. She didn't say anything. No one said anything. For several moments, the playground was, once again, strangely quiet.

"Tug-of-war," Saeed said. "We could play tug-of-war!"

"Great idea," Donut said.

Maude still didn't say anything.

"Are you chicken?" Donut asked. "Too chicken to play tug-of-war?"

"Don't say anything bad about chickens!"

Maude said, getting her voice back. "Chickens are the greatest bird of all! We *will* play tug-of-war. And we'll beat you! Girls versus boys!" She picked up one end of the rope and slid it to Hillary, who passed it to Miranda, who passed it to Desdemona, who hesitated but dropped her soccer ball to pass it to Agatha, who passed it to Agnes.

The boys picked up the other end.

"Wait!" Hillary hollered. "We need an impartial referee."

"I'll do it," said one of the littlest children, who was standing at the very edge of the sandbox. The boy was very small with extraordinarily large ears and a backpack that looked like it weighed more than he did.

Everyone was surprised. Had he been there the whole time?

"I never take sides," the boy said seriously. "I can't. I have four older brothers and five younger sisters."

The big-eared boy was an excellent choice, because the first thing he did was take a ruler out of his backpack and measure Maude's rope. Then

he drew a line on the ground with a piece of chalk and made sure that each team was the same distance from it. Then he put on a referee shirt, hung a whistle around his neck, and explained the rules. Finally, he blew his whistle and said, "Begin!"

The boys pulled hard. The girls pulled harder.

"Hold your ground!" Hillary shouted.

"Toe the line!" Felix panted. "I mean, keep your toe *behind* the line."

"Girls rule, boys drool," Desdemona said.

"Boys rule, girls drool," Norris shouted back.

"Tug!" Maude screamed. "Tug your hearts out, ladies!"

"Keep going, boys!" Donut cried.

"Take no prisoners!" Maude shouted.

"No pain, no gain!" Saeed yelled.

"Don't give up the ship!" Hillary commanded as her left toe inched slightly closer to the chalk line.

"Never surrender!" Donut screamed.

Prisoners, Miranda wondered. *Ship? Pain? Surrender? Weren't they playing a game?*

"Remember, failure is . . ." Maude chanted, trying to remember the last word of the quote her dad had told her that morning. Susan B. Anthony, the social reformer, had said, "Failure is . . ." Maude couldn't remember. Her dad told her so many quotes, she sometimes got them jumbled. "Failure is . . ." Maude said again, trying desperately to remember.

"Impossible!" Hillary screeched as she turned to look at Maude and, in doing so, loosened her grip, which let the boys pull her big toe across the line.

Fweeeeeeeeeeeeeet! The big-eared referee blew his whistle. "The team to my left has officially crossed the demarcation line at thirteen hundred hours." He sounded official.

"Ha ha!" the boys hooted.

"It was that Susan B. Anthony quote," Hillary whined. "If you'd remembered the last word was *impossible*, I wouldn't have turned around to tell you!"

"Ugh," Maude grumbled, both because they'd lost and because it was such a silly word to have forgotten.

The boys shouted, "We won! Boys beat girls! Boys beat girls!"

"Don't worry, girls," Maude said. "I'll come up

with something. I'll organize the greatest plan in the world. The boys won't win."

From their side of the rope, the girls glared at the boys. The boys glared back. And then the bell rang, so everyone went back inside.

12

NO MORE CHICKENS

The first thing Maude did when she got home that tug-of-war Tuesday was scoop up her beloved Frizzle chicken, Rosalie, who was waiting on the bottom step outside the house. Rosalie was the official house chicken, but due to her peeing in the house, Maude's dad, Walt, and her brother, Michael-John, had officially declared that she could only be in the house when Maude was there, too. That way Maude would always be around to clean up.

"My loveliest ladybird!" Maude sang. "There's nothing chicken about you except that you're a chicken!"

"Maude!" Michael-John called out of an open window. Her brother was already home, because he was homeschooled. "Bring up the newspaper. Dad wants it."

Maude nodded, tucked Rosalie into her armpit,

grabbed the newspaper, and bounded up the twenty-seven slightly crooked steps into her house.

"I am home," she announced. "Here's your paper of news." She handed Walt the *Mountain River Valley News* and bowed. Rosalie, still under her arm, squawked.

"Many thanks, my beautiful biscuit beetle," Walt said, taking the paper. "As the poet 'Stanislaw' Jerzy Lec said, 'The window to the world can be covered by a newspaper.'"

"'Stanislaw' would make an excellent chicken name." Maude looked at her dad hopefully.

"No more chickens," Walt and Michael-John said.

"And don't let that chicken near my dictionaries, Maude." Michael-John pointed to one of his dictionaries, which lay open on the windowsill. "Rosalie peed on all the *p* pages."

"Maybe she's learning to read," Maude said hopefully.

Her brother gave her a look.

"I'm training her," Maude said. "I'm reading a long book about it." She whispered into what she thought was her chicken's ear, "Let me know if you have to pee."

"How was school?" Walt asked.

"School . . ." Maude said, as if she'd forgotten where she'd been all day. She thought for a minute. The removal of the swings and losing tug-of-war had been horribly horrible, but on the plus side, now the other 3B girls were just as mad at the boys as she was. And because she had so much social justice experience, she would naturally be their leader. "School was school," Maude said. "Some good parts and some extremely not-so-good parts."

"I like the good parts. Do you want to talk about the extremely not-so-good parts?"

"No can do," Maude said. "I'm too busy. The people look to me for a plan!"

For the rest of the afternoon, Maude tried to come up with a plan. She took several breaks to sing to her chicken, ignore her homework, walk her beloved dog, Rudolph Valentino, scratch her cat behind his ears, eat dinner, and crush both Walt and Michael-John in a vicious game of Parcheesi. It wasn't until she got into bed that she remembered she was supposed to be planning, and then she promptly fell asleep without a plan. (And without brushing her teeth!)

But, much to her delight, after an odd dream about Susan B. Anthony, a poet, a chicken, and a very heavy newspaper, when she woke up, she had one!

13

THE *GIRLS GAZETTE*

"We're starting a newspaper," Maude told the girls Wednesday morning before the first bell rang. They were sitting with their backs against the fence as far as they could get from the boys, who were once again at the sandbox on the other side of the playground. Desdemona, Agnes, and Agatha, afraid their soccer balls would be the next to go, sat on them.

"A newspaper?" Desdemona asked.

"Yes! A one-hundred-percent-official, girls-only newspaper!" Maude saluted the air. "As long as the castle has a printing press. It does, right?" She looked at Miranda.

"I think so," Miranda said. "Are printing presses very large with ink fountains and grippers?"

Maude nodded. "Excellent! You're the publisher."

"Why a newspaper?" Agnes asked.

Maude jumped up onto the rusty lunch box that had somehow traveled across the playground. "Freedom of the press! The power of print! It will be by women, about women, and for women! And by women, I mean girls only!" Just as Maude finished her speech, the bell rang, so the girls ran to line up.

"The boys won't have anything to do with it?" Miranda asked as they walked inside.

Maude grinned. "Not. A. Thing."

"But Norbert's the best writer in class, Saeed is amazing at punctuation, and Donut . . ."

Maude shook her head. "Norbert is a *story* writer. And playwright. We're going to write *news*."

"What kind of news?" Hillary asked.

"News about the boys cheating at tug-of-war, how dumb tag is, stuff like that!"

"Thinking tag is dumb is an opinion," Miranda said as they walked into class.

But Maude, who was poking Hillary on the back, didn't seem to hear.

"Hillary, you'd make a great managing editor," Maude said. "What do you say?"

"I'm too busy balancing." Hillary sat down at her desk.

"Being a managing editor is perfect for balancing. Managing editors come up with the articles that the reporters, *girl* reporters, report. And they make sure everyone meets their deadlines. It's nothing but balancing!"

"I'll consider it," Hillary said.

Maude jumped up on her desk, glared at the boys, and whispered, "We'll be like the great women who started *The Una*, the first women's rights newspaper ever published! They called it 'a paper devoted to the elevation of women.' How awesome is that?"

"Maude? What are you doing?" Miss Kinde asked sweetly.

"Um . . . elevating?"

"Well, please save your elevating for recess."

Maude nodded and slid back into her seat.

"We'll go down in Mountain River Valley Elementary School history," Maude whispered.

Hillary considered this. "Okay. I'll do it. Now let me start my practice exam so I can beat you."

"Hooray!" Maude shouted. "Hooray for the *Girls Gazette!*"

"Maude!" Miss Kinde gave her a rare I'm-the-teacher-you're-the-student look.

"Sorry," Maude said sincerely. She picked up her pencil and tried to focus on her exam, but her mind was buzzing with excitement, knowing the

Girls Gazette would totally prove that the 3B girls were so much better than the boys!

14

THE LIST OF WEEKLY EVENTS AND OTHER IMPORTANT ARTICLES

Led by Maude Brandywine Mayhew Kaye, editor in chief, the staff of the *Girls Gazette* had their first official meeting during recess.

"I just thought of a great story," Agatha said after Maude had given a thankfully short but very good speech on the historical importance of newspapers. "I saw Norbert and Fletcher in the grocery store yesterday. And guess what?"

"I know," Maude said. "They tripped an old lady with a cane! They threw soup cans at a baby!"

"Maude!" Miranda sounded horrified. "Norbert and Fletcher would never do that." Just last week, she'd seen Fletcher take a kindergartener with extremely bloody knees to the nurse.

"They crashed in the fruit aisle," Agatha said excitedly. "A million bananas fell down! Maybe

they were play-
ing tag."

"The dan-
gers of tag,"
Maude said
excitedly. "That could be the lead story! 'Above
the fold,' as they say in the news biz!"

"But we don't know they were playing tag,"
Miranda said quietly.

"I'm sure they were." Maude sounded
confident.

"I'll interview myself about the injury I got when
Donut knocked me over," Hillary said. "I'll give long
answers to my long questions."

Maude nodded.

"What about cartoons?" Desdemona shifted
on the soccer ball she was sitting on. "My grandpa
says that's the only good part of the paper. I can
draw everything but horses, hands, and bicycles."

"Excellent," Maude said.

"What about me?" Agnes asked. "I hate writing
and can't draw."

"Well, um . . ." Maude didn't want to force

anyone to join the paper, but she thought that for the *Girls Gazette* to be a true movement, all 3B girls should be involved.

"But I'm the second-best speller in the class and always know where commas go. Could I do that?"

Maude breathed a sigh of relief. "You'll make a terrific copy editor, Agnes."

"What about Miss Kinde?" Miranda asked. "Should we ask her to write something?"

"No," Maude said.

"But she *was* a girl," Miranda said. "Before she was a grown-up."

"Yes, but look." Maude pointed to their teacher, who was somehow giving Saeed an ice pack with one hand while tying Fletcher's shoelace with the other. "Does Miss Kinde need to know about the *Girls Gazette*?"

The girls looked at one another. *Should the* Girls Gazette *be a secret?*

"She already has so much work. She doesn't need more." Maude sounded concerned.

Since none of the girls wanted to give their beloved teacher more work, they moved on.

"Advertising," Hillary said, looking at the list on her clipboard. "A paper needs ads."

Maude nodded. "We'll advertise the next *Girls Gazette* staff meeting. And make an ad for pet vaccination. Whether your animal is a boy or a girl, pet vaccination is important."

"You'll check on the printing press?" Hillary asked Miranda.

Miranda nodded.

"Everyone must meet their deadline," Hillary said. "I'm very busy. Mostly with balancing, but there's also all the extra homework I like to do and my tuba lessons and extra practice-exam practice and yo-yo club and my cotton-ball craft group and my difficult-book club and my granny is coming to visit . . ." She trailed off, overwhelmed by how much she had to do.

"I just had yet another brilliant idea!" Maude shouted. "The *Girls Gazette* will have a list of weekly events. A list of everything that's going on. But just for the girls, of course! Like your balance competition." She looked at Hillary, who was standing on one leg with the clipboard on her head.

"I have a soccer game Saturday morning," Desdemona said. "And a gymnastics jamboree Saturday afternoon!"

"That will be listed," Maude said.

"My birthday is next Tuesday," Agnes said.

Maude nodded.

"I'm going to my cousin's birthday party on Sunday," Agatha said. "Ellis Fredrick von Miltenberger the Third is going to be five. Or maybe six. Possibly seventeen. I don't know, actually."

"Sorry," Maude said. "The *Girls Gazette* is girls only. No matter how old he is, Ellis Fredrick von Miltenberger's birthday won't make the list."

Agatha looked sad but then perked up. "I'm going to my aunt's baby shower soon. She's having two girls!"

"Excellent," Maude said. "Two girls can definitely be in the list of weekly events!"

15

NEWSPAPERS ARE REALLY A LOT OF WORK

For the rest of the week, before school, during recess, during school, and after school, the girls of 3B secretly worked on the *Girls Gazette*.

It turned out that putting out a newspaper was really hard. Articles were written and rewritten. Cartoons were drawn and redrawn. Vast quantities of pretzels were eaten. Commas were put in. Spelling mistakes were found, corrected, and then corrected again. Commas were taken out. Finally, late Thursday evening, when every *i* was dotted and every *t* crossed, Maude and Miranda set out to print.

Even with KD's assistance, printing a newspaper proved extremely time consuming and complicated. The press required a great deal of ink, and ink turned out to be quite messy. In the end, Maude and Miranda stayed up way past

their school-night bedtimes in order to get the
paper out on schedule.

Early Friday morning, before Miss Kinde
came in, the exhausted girls of 3B proudly put
a copy of their paper on every boy's desk. They
had done it! It was officially in print that tag was

the worst game ever and that the girls were better than the boys at training chickens, balancing,
playing soccer, skateboarding, and practically
everything else!

The boys got very quiet when they came into their classroom that Friday. And then, one by one, they began to read.

Tag Is Really Stupid and Incredibly Dangerous: by Editor in Chief Maude Brandywine Mayhew Kaye the First

How I Injured My Leg: An Interview with and by Hillary Greenlight-Miller, Managing Editor

Doughnuts Are the Worst Dessert in the World: by Maude Kaye, Cartoons by Desdemona Mallet

Really Cool Things That Happened to the Really Cool Girls of 3B!

Agnes lost her tooth and found her lost library book on the same day!

Desdemona almost scored a goal at soccer. Agatha stayed on her skateboard for three minutes.

Hillary is the best balancer in the whole school.

Hillary beat her personal best on last week's practice exam.

Maude beat her personal best and Hillary's personal best on last week's practice exam.

Miranda found the perfect end table for the West Library.

Maude has mostly trained her chicken to mostly not pee in the house.

Friday: Hillary has balance practice; Maude's dog, cat, and chicken have appointments at the vet for vaccinations; Agnes and Agatha are having a two-night sleepover.

Saturday: Desdemona has her soccer game at 10:00 a.m.; Hillary has balance practice.

Sunday: Hillary has balance practice; Agatha is playing piano at the senior center.

Monday: Hillary has balance practice and a dentist appointment.

Tuesday: Agnes's birthday! Miranda has extra early-morning help with Miss Kinde.

Wednesday: *Girls Gazette* staff meeting during recess; Agnes has a piano lesson; Hillary has balance practice; Miranda has to go to a royally boring dinner party.

Thursday: Hillary has balance practice; Miranda has extra-extra early-morning help with Miss Kinde.

16

THE SECOND BOYS–ONLY MEETING

Hunched over his desk reading the *Girls Gazette*, Donut fumed. *Tag is not stupid*, he thought. Doughnuts were the best dessert, not the worst! Hillary's leg was fine! She could stand on one leg better than anyone. And the impartial referee had impartially said the boys had won tug-of-war fair and square! *How could the girls write all this stuff?* Donut stayed furious while taking his morning practice exam; during music, where he purposely played his recorder extra off-key; and at lunch, where he mindlessly swallowed bits of flavorless cafeteria food. It wasn't until recess, when he was hitting a pile of sand with a stick, that inspiration struck: the boys would have a newspaper too! And it would be better, so much better, than the *Girls Gazette*!

"Boys-only meeting," Donut whispered loudly. "I have an idea!" He took the *Girls Gazette* out of his pocket. "We're going to make a newspaper too! And it's going to be better. Much better!"

"How?" Felix asked. "We don't have a printing press."

"But who prints the town paper?" Donut asked.

Felix looked blank and then smacked his palm on his forehead. "Oh! Right! My dad! The *Mountain River Valley News*. 'From the mountain to the river to the valley, we print the news!'"

"So he must have printers."

Felix nodded. "There's a building of them at the bottom of Mount Coffee."

Donut grinned. "And Norris, isn't your mom a world-famous photographer?"

Norris nodded.

"She probably has a lot of cameras."

Norris nodded again.

"Can you take pictures?"

Norris nodded a third and final time.

"And my great-uncle Jacoby is the town mailman," Fletcher said eagerly.

The boys looked at him. *What did great-uncle Jacoby have to do with a newspaper?*

"So," Fletcher said, "not only can we print a *real* newspaper with *real* photographs, we can get them *delivered!*" He laughed. "To everyone! Not just Three B. I'm sure he'd be happy to make an extra early delivery for his favorite great-nephew!"

The boys grinned! Their paper would be better and bigger and way more awesome than the *Girls Gazette*.

17

THE *BOYS BUGLE*

The girls of 3B spent the weekend doing the activities listed in the *Girls Gazette* weekly events list. Desdemona soccered and gymnasticked. Hillary balanced and did eight million other things. Miranda and Maude helped Walt make not-salty-enough salt bread. Agnes and Agatha did not get nearly enough sleep at their two-night sleepover, which meant that Agatha was so tired by the time she arrived at the senior center for her performance, she fell asleep while playing "The Blue Danube." The seniors clapped anyway.

The boys of 3B, on the other hand, canceled their weekend plans. There were no origami clubs or calligraphy classes. There was no karate or water polo. There was no doing nothing except reading comics and eating bowls of pepperoni on the couch.

The boys spent their weekend working on the *Boys Bugle*.

They took notes. They took pictures. They wrote. They rewrote. They drank chocolate milk. They designed. They argued over headlines. They argued over commas. They redesigned. They drank more chocolate milk. They changed headlines. They ran out of chocolate milk, so they drank warm pineapple juice, which was disgusting. They spell-checked. And then, finally, at the latest possible hour on Sunday night, they were done.

"It's amazing," Norbert said proudly.

"Best of the best," Norris said.

"The girls are going to be so mad," Donut said, beaming.

18

THE *BOYS BUGLE* DELIVERED

"Well, this is interesting," KD said, walking into the royal breakfast nook on Monday morning.

Miranda looked up from her breakfast. Her dad was holding the *Mountain River Valley News* and something called the *Boys Bugle*.

Across town, Walt walked into the kitchen with two newspapers, too.

"Well, this is curious," Walt said, opening the *Boys Bugle*. "Some of your classmates were busy this weekend." He sounded impressed.

Maude stared at the newspaper her father held out. It was not the *Girls Gazette* or the *Mountain River Valley News*. But it was thick, with beautiful color pictures. Plus, it had been delivered! Right to her house! And the lead article was called "Tag Is Officially the Best Game Ever and the Boys Did Not Cheat at Tug-of-War"!

THE BOYS BUGLE

*Tag Is Officially the Best Game Ever and the Boys Did
Not Cheat at Tug-of-War!*
By: Duncan David "Donut" Donatello,
Norris Zipper, and Felix E. Chang

It set accunti toris coloraroro coraro omnis anamodita et facoqod quis alit ras saqua quataconti nam vanda saqoina antam vid modis sit ancat dolaptatimquo coloraqro arom la ons antamotam colori dolorqo ramporsqo dolapta aqarom atoribus anplit aptatia nus, nacoqardarum soluptatanisunti toris coloraroro coraro omnis anamodita et facoqod quis alit ras saqua quataconti nam vanda saqoina antam vid modis sit ancat dolaptatimquo coloraqro arom la ons antamotam colori dolorqo ramporsqo dolapta aqarom atoribus anplit aptatia nus, nacoqardarum soluptatanis plataniconti toris coloraroro coraro omnis anamodita et facoqod quis alit ras saqua quataconti nam vanda saqoina antam vid modis sit ancat dolaptatimquo coloraqro arom la ons antamotam colori dolorqo ramporsqo dolapta aqarom atoribus anplit aptatia nus, nacoqardarum soluptatanis ramporsqo dolapta aqarom atoribus anplit aptatia nus, nacoqardarum soluptatanisunti toris coloraroro coraro omnis anamodita et facoqod quis alit ras saqua quataconti nam vanda saqoina antam vid modis sit ancat dolaptatimquo coloraqro arom la ons antamotam colori dolorqo ramporsqo dolapta aqarom atoribus anplit aptatia nus, nacoqardarum soluptatanis plataniconti toris coloraroro coraro omnis anamodita et facoqod quis alit ras saqua quataca

Balancing: Is It Really That Hard? By Fletcher Diamond

mparsqo dolapta aqarom atoribus anplit aptatia nus, nacoqardarum soluptatanisunti toris coloraroro coraro omnis anamodita et facoqod quis alit ras saqua quataconti nam vanda saqoina antam vid modis sit ancat dolaptatimquo coloraqro arom la ons antamotam colori dolorqo ramporsqo dolapta aqarom atoribus anplit aptatia nus, nacoqardarum soluptatanis plataniconti toris coloraroro coraro omnis anamodita et facoqod quis alit ras saqua quataconti nam vanda saqoina antam vid modis sit ancat dolaptatimquo coloraqro arom la ons antamotam colori dolorqo ramporsqo dolapta

Even Cooler Things That Happened to the Even Cooler Boys of 3B!

- Donut baked doughnuts that were so good his mom thought they were from the store.

- Norris passed his yellow belt test, lost a tooth, and was student of the day all on the same day.

- Fletcher got 100 PERCENT on his spelling test and he didn't even study.

- Norbert wrote 200 words in one day!

- Felix can pogo stick backward without hands.

- Saeed cannot lose at rock paper scissors.

BOYS' EVENTS

MONDAY

Donut yo-yo club | **Fletcher** origami lesson | **Felix** dentist appt.

TUESDAY

Norris dentist appt. | **Felix** carpentry class | **Saeed** drum lesson

WEDNESDAY

Norbert comic book club | **Saeed** band practice | **Fletcher** dentist appt. | **Norris** swim meet

THURSDAY

Saeed Tae kwon do | **Norbert** viola lesson | **Donut** dentist appt.

FRIDAY

Fletcher and **Felix** sleepover extravaganza! | **Saeed** dentist appt.

SATURDAY

Norbert and **Norris** and **Saeed** and **Donut** soccer practice | **Fletcher** allergy shots | **Felix** hockey tickets!

SUNDAY

Norbert needs to get a new suit, which will probably be itchy and tight | **Donut** has to go to a boring lunch with his mom's friends, who always say he's getting really big and ask what grade he's in | **Saeed** has to play with his annoying little cousins who drool a lot and make everything sticky

MAUDE CALLS AN EMERGENCY MEETING

"Meeting!" Maude announced when she got to the playground Monday morning.

"Our meeting isn't until recess." Agatha didn't look up from the *Boys Bugle*. "That's how it's listed in the *Girls Gazette*."

"*The Boys Bugle* has a real calendar. Not just a list," Hillary said. "It looks cool."

"*Emergency* meeting," Maude said loudly. "We can't stand for this!"

"Stand for what?" Miranda asked.

"For the *Boys Bugle*! It isn't fair."

"Why isn't it fair?" Miranda was confused. "We made a paper, they made a paper."

"It's . . . it's . . ." Maude said. "They took our idea. And they . . ." She didn't say anything else, but everyone knew what she was thinking: *The boys took our idea and made it better!*

"But your dad told us that quote," Miranda said. "Remember when you got mad after your brother copied the shape of your bread and your dad said that quote about imitation and flattery. Shouldn't we be flattered that the boys made a paper, too?"

"Charles Caleb Colton said, 'Imitation is the sincerest form of flattery,'" Maude said. "But we should *not* be flattered. We should be furious!"

You certainly look furious, Miranda thought. Maude was sweaty and red. And her hair was sticking up in more ways than ever.

"Those boys must be punished for their crime!" Maude declared.

It's not a crime, Miranda thought. *It's freedom of the press. At least, I think it is.* She looked at Maude curiously. Was she missing something? After all, she hadn't been in school as long as Maude. And Maude knew a lot more quotes and wore a lot of buttons.

"But what can we do?" Agnes asked.

Maude jumped back onto the rusty lunchbox and cleared her throat. "The boys might have beaten us at tug-of-war and newspapering.

They might have taken our swings and balance beam. Our soccer balls might be in great danger! But they can't outsmart us." Maude tapped her temple. "And that is why I stand here before you not only as editor in chief but also as your commander."

"Commander?" the girls said.

Maude nodded. "I hereby officially accept the position of commander in the battle of wits!"

"What battle of wits?" Desdemona asked.

Maude cleared her throat. "We're going to beat them with our brains."

The girls nodded. Using their brains was definitely a smart idea.

"How?" Hillary asked.

"Agnes, your birthday is tomorrow, right?" Maude asked. "That's listed in our weekly events."

Agnes grinned. "I'm bringing tiny cupcakes!"

"No, you're not," Maude said matter-of-factly. "You're bringing doughnuts. Large doughnuts."

"Large doughnuts?" Agnes frowned. "Tiny cupcakes are much better than large doughnuts."

"Yes," Maude said. "I agree, but trust me."

VERY EARLY TUESDAY MORNING

Extremely early Tuesday morning, at the moment the sun was changing places with the moon, a student in 3B got to work. The student checked their supplies and nodded. *Revenge would be sweet*, the student thought.

DONUT GETS A DOUGHNUT

At the scheduled birthday-celebration time, Agnes passed out doughnuts. As planned ahead of time, she gave the largest one to Donut.

"Oh, boy," Donut said gleefully. He took an enormous bite and happily chewed, savoring the sweet dough and waiting for the tangy jelly to ooze into his mouth. Donut kept chewing. Where was the jelly? This wasn't like any jelly dough-nut he'd had before. He tried to swallow, but his mouth felt stuck. And then Donut realized: there was no jelly! There was . . . *What was in the doughnut?*

"Is he okay?" Miranda pointed to Donut, whose eyes were big and full of panic. Also, there was a very unusual, horribly strong smell in 3B. Miranda sniffed and looked at Maude.

Maude grinned. "I don't know what you're talking about," she said.

Miranda sniffed again and looked back at Donut. Did the battle of wits have something to do with Donut's doughnut? Was that why Maude wouldn't let Agnes bring tiny cupcakes? The smell in the room was getting so strong that any second now she was sure Miss Kinde would open the windows. *The smell*, Miranda thought, *is almost worse than hard-boiled eggs and the gymnasium combined.* The classroom smelled like sweat and feet and . . . cheese! *Maude's cheese,* Miranda thought, remembering Maude's half-eaten sandwich that had fallen out of her bag the other day.

Miranda looked over at Maude, but Maude, busy eating her doughnut and reading her chicken-training book, didn't notice.

Without thinking too much about it, Miranda took out a piece of pink paper and, in her neatest and smallest handwriting, wrote: Cheese. (Limburger, I think.)

Heart pounding, Miranda quickly dropped the note on Donut's desk.

Donut, who still hadn't swallowed, noticed the note right away.

"Cheese," he read. *Cheese?*

And then, in the midst of the worst doughnut experience of his life, Donut understood. The jelly in his jelly doughnut was not jelly! It was cheese! And not just any cheese. The smelliest, most disgusting, sweaty-feet-tasting cheese in the entire universe. But what could he do?

"Blgrrrehhhammmm!" Donut spit out the whole disgusting mess into a mountainous heap on his desk.

Everyone stared at Donut.

"Donut?" Miss Kinde said.

Donut opened his mouth, but he didn't know what to say. Also, he had to get over his embarrassment, stand up, get some paper towels, and clean his desk.

"Thanks for the delicious doughnuts, Agnes," Maude said loudly. She winked at Miranda.

Miranda, who didn't like sweets, looked at her uneaten non-cheese doughnut. Maude might be her best friend, but right now Miranda felt too bad or maybe too sad or maybe too mad to wink back.

Donut looked at his disgusting desk and felt madder than ever.

But then he noticed a curly feather on the floor. It must have fallen out of Maude's bag. And suddenly, even though he had the worst taste in his mouth, Donut had the best idea ever!

22

VERY EARLY WEDNESDAY MORNING

Extremely early Wednesday morning, at the moment the sun was changing places with the moon, a student in 3B got to work. The student checked their supplies and nodded. *Revenge*, the student thought. *Revenge, revenge, revenge!*

23

WHERE'S ROSALIE?

Wednesday morning, Maude hollered through the megaphone she'd borrowed from Hillary, "EMERGENCY MEETING!"

Everyone on the playground stared at her.

"EMERGENCY MEETING FOR THE GIRLS OF THREE B," she corrected.

The girls of 3B followed Maude over to where the swings had been.

"A terrible crime has been committed," Maude told them. "I discovered early this morning that my best and only Frizzle chicken, Ms. Rosalie Esmerelda Clementina Pickled Beets Kaye, has been . . . STOLEN!"

The girls gasped. "Stolen?" they said.

"Are you sure?" Miranda asked.

"Positive. When I went outside to get her for breakfast, she was gone!"

"Isn't she a house chicken?" Desdemona asked.

"Yes," Maude said. "But her limited bathroom skills limit her house time. She slept outside last night. It's not important. What's important is that I looked everywhere! In the coop, in the tire swing, in the mailbox. Then I wondered if she'd snuck into the house—she does that sometimes—so I looked in all of the cabinets and closets. I looked in every drawer and under every desk. I looked under books and beds and in a briefcase."

"How could a chicken be in a briefcase?" Agatha asked.

"Never mind," Maude said. "Trust me, Rosalie is gone!"

"Perhaps she flew the coop," Hillary said. "Took a vacation."

"Rosalie can't fly," Maude said. "She just sort of jumps. And chickens don't take vacations."

"Maybe—" Agnes said.

But Maude stopped her. "I know one of the boys from Three B stole my favorite chicken. And we're going to prove it."

No one said anything.

"Do you know how we're going to solve the great chicken-napping?" Maude asked.

The girls shook their heads.

"With the next issue of the *Girls Gazette*! Our second issue will dig deeper, be more investigative!" Maude took the rusty lunchbox out of her bag and stood on it. "Plus, this time we'll have color photographs, and I'll ask the little kids who used to hang out at the sandbox to deliver it."

For a long time, nobody said anything. Hillary looked at Agnes, who looked at Agatha, who looked at Desdemona, who looked at Miranda, who looked at her sparkly shoes.

Finally, Hillary spoke. "Sorry, Maude," she said. "I'm sorry about your chicken, but what you did to Donut's doughnut was really gross. I'm done with the news biz. Being managing editor took too much time. Since there's no balance beam on the playground, I have to practice more after school."

Agnes nodded. "If I'd known why you wanted doughnuts, I never would've done it!"

"Yeah," Desdemona said. "My grandpa laughed so hard at my cartoons he cried. Not because they were funny. Because the hands I drew were so bad! So, no more cartoons until I can draw hands."

"It turns out that I actually don't know anything about commas," Agnes said. "My mom said I need extra comma help from Miss Kinde after school."

"What?" Maude sounded angry. "What happened to my recess rebels?"

"I want regular recess," Agatha said. "I'm done rebelling."

"You're our friend, but we don't want you as commander anymore," Desdemona said.

"But—" Maude sputtered. "But my chicken is stolen, and none of you will help?"

"I'll help you look for her," Miranda said softly.

"But will you publish the *Girls Gazette* issue two?" Maude asked. "Or are you surrendering the fort like everyone else?"

Miranda didn't know what to do. On the one hand, Miranda agreed with the other girls that Maude had been wrong to sneak cheese into Donut's doughnut. On the other hand, Maude's beloved chicken was missing, possibly stolen! And they were best friends! Wasn't friendship the most important thing of all?

"I'll print it," Miranda said after a long pause. "If you write it, I can print it."

24

MAUDE CAN'T PROVE IT

Try as she might, Maude couldn't prove that one of the boys in 3B had stolen her chicken. She couldn't interview the boys without talking to them—and she was planning on never speaking to them again. To take her mind off her missing chicken and the fact that she'd been fired as commander, Maude focused on the second issue of the *Girls Gazette*.

Without any other reporters, she did the reporting herself. The first story was easy, because it was all about Rosalie. Then she described, in great detail, how delicious Agnes's birthday doughnuts had been and how disgusting it was that Donut had rudely spit his out.

Then she copied the pet vaccination ad from the first issue.

But after that, she was stuck. She looked at Onion the Great Number Eleven for inspiration.

"I could write about your missing eye," Maude told the cat. "That was such a good, gruesome story." But what did a cat's eye have to do with the girls in 3B? *Nothing*, Maude thought sadly. "I wish I had more gruesome stories about the boys," she said.

And then Maude remembered something that had happened a long time ago. It wasn't gruesome, but maybe it was interesting. And possibly extremely embarrassing. Maude hesitated but then wrote it all down. After that, in a fantastic burst of inspiration, Maude wrote down a bunch of other possibly interesting, extremely embarrassing stories!

25

GIRLS GAZETTE ISSUE TWO

Late the following Monday afternoon, Maude delivered the second issue of the *Girls Gazette* to the castle. "Sorry I'm so late," she panted as she burst into the printing-press room. "It's amazing I made the deadline without a staff."

Miranda nodded, truly impressed that Maude had written an entire paper by herself.

"Can you run the press alone?" Maude asked. "I'd help, but now that the paper is done, I must continue to search for my chicken."

"Okay," Miranda said. She wasn't excited to print all by herself, but she knew a deal was a deal.

"Let's print three hundred more copies this time. We can't deliver them, because the sand-box kids said they're not allowed to walk around town by themselves. But we can give copies to *all* the boys at school, not just the boys in our class."

"You want three hundred *more* copies?"

"Yup!"

Miranda yawned. Just thinking about how late she'd have to stay up to print that many papers made her exhausted.

"Thank you," Maude said. "I'm going to look for Rosalie now."

"Good luck," Miranda said. "I hope you find her." *And good luck to me*, she thought, *for agreeing to be publisher on another school night!*

After Maude left, Miranda wished that KD wasn't at a royal ribbon-cutting ceremony. She knew he'd help her when he got home, but she figured she should get started or they'd be up all night. She was putting on her printing apron when she heard a strange chirping noise from the direction of the Unknown Forest. She put her ear against the window. What was it? Was one of the castle's ducks in trouble? She looked down and counted all eight ducks in the moat below.

Miranda looked away from the ducks and picked up the *Girls Gazette* issue two. She glanced at the main story, which was about the stolen chicken. Miranda nodded. That was certainly news! But then she glanced at the story below it and blinked. She took off her glasses and rubbed her eyes. She must be tired. She put her glasses back on. But no. The story was still there: "Donut Peed His Pants in Kindergarten!"

GIRLS GAZETTE

Where Is Rosalie?

If all assunti toris colorcoro coraro sunts anamaditas at facaqed quis alis ros sequa quatacanti nam vanda saquina coram vid modis sit ances doloyta

Agnes's Birthday Doughnuts Were Really Delicious and It Was So Revolting When Donut Rudely Spit His Out!

Uytafor, inullantiat illaytat raisini actorantotas aassimus masimut arfarsyarrom rorilus nus doloytasyaraSi coofator saqua vandaarilus som a natam unt arum iundam faqit, suntis rit angland ipistrum vara non ga yarum nohitatin nonsact iandis ut lam inimi, yandiotya anorum quia vallandundi sumi volo corrum sandiccior, aus alitus sumyuos volaro molorator?

Norris Sleeps with a Disgusting Stuffed Pig

If all assunti toris colorcoro coraro sunts anamaditas at facaqed quis alis ros sequa quatacanti nam vanda saquina coram vid modis sit ances doloyta

Saeed Farted in Music Class!

sdaytaqua sunti doloraya dolit narstia at quo us doloris nraqidotiX attam sonsat lab. Naquia vallorram sanca yra andam ut at ipsandas idiation ranibit modi andas.

Donut Sleeps with Two Nightlights!

Uytafor, inullantiat illaytat raisini actorantotas aassimus masimut arfarsyarrom rorilus nus doloytasyaraca

Felix Can't Watch Scary Tv

Uytafor, inullantiat illaytat raisini actorantotas aassimus masimut arfarsyarrom rorilus nus doloytasyaraSi coofator saqua vandaarilus som a natam unt arum iundam faqit, suntis rit angland ipistrum vara non ga yarum nohitatin nonsact iandis ut lam inimi, yandiotya anorum quia vallandundi sumi volo corrum sandiccior, aus alitus sumyuos volaro molorator?

Donut Peed His Pants in Kindergarten!

If all assunti toris colorcoro coraro sunts anamaditas at facaqed quis alis ros sequa quatacanti nam vanda saquina coram vid modis sit ances doloytafuuqua voloraya arum la cus cucamram colori doloryo ramqartya doloyta aparum atorilus anqit aytatia uytafor, inullantiat illaytat raisini actorantotas aassimus masimut arfarsyarrom rorilus nus doloytasyaraSi coofator saqua vandaarilus som a natam unt arum iundam faqit, suntis rit angland ipistrum vara non ga yarum nohitatin nonsact iandis ut lam inimi, yandiotya anorum quia vallandundi sumi volo nis uytafor, inullantiat illaytat raisini actorantotas aassimuarfarsyarrom rorilus nus doloytasyaraSi coofator saqua vandaarilus som a natam unt arum iundam faqit, suntis rit angland ipistrum vara non ga yarum nohitatin nonsact iandis ut lam inimi, yandiotya anorum quia vallandundi sumi volo corrum sandiccior, aus alitus sumyuos volaro molorator?

Norbert's Mom Still Calls Him "Baby"

If all assunti toris colorcoro coraro sunts anamaditas at facaqed quis alis ros sequa quatacanti nam vanda saquina coram vid modis sit ances doloytafuuqua voloraya arum la cus cucamram colori doloryo ramqartya doloyta aparum atorilus anqit aytatia nus, nacuyarfarum doloytatatis doloytatiti ant volland amquaa yorant adit, iqtant atur, officiis as authotacnars il anto ma

Fletcher Had to Call His Dad to Pick Him Up at a Sleepover Because He Was Scared

26

MIRANDA WONDERS WHAT TO DO

Miranda read the second issue of the *Girls Gazette* cover to cover. Then she read it again. Then she sat down on a small footstool next to the printing press and put her head in her hands.

She didn't know what to do.

The second issue of the *Girls Gazette* was nothing like the first. The first issue had mostly great things about the girls, while the second issue, with the exception of the story about Rosalie and the ad for pet vaccination, had nothing but truly terrible things about the boys. Miranda wouldn't feel proud printing three hundred and sixteen copies of this newspaper. She would feel . . . how would she feel? *Truly terrible*, she thought. How did Maude know Fletcher's dad had picked him up at a sleepover? And anyone could have farted during music! There was no way Maude could know it had been Saeed. Was Maude making this stuff up? Even if the story about Donut was true, why would Maude write about something that had happened so long ago? Maude herself slept with an enormous group of stuffed animals and part of an ancient baby blanket mysteriously called Todd. Miranda had QM sing her to sleep most nights, and even though she wasn't really embarrassed by that, she certainly didn't want it in the paper! Wasn't a newspaper supposed to print *news*?

Miranda's head began to ache the way it had before she'd gotten glasses. If Miranda told Maude she wouldn't publish issue two, Maude would give a brilliant speech with a million reasons and quotes about why she should. If Miranda *did* print it . . . Miranda didn't want to think about what would happen then. She leaned her face on the cool window and looked out at the grounds below. Maybe she should check on the ducks after all. Perhaps she'd counted wrong.

She walked out of the printing-press room, down a flight of winding steps, and onto a narrow path above the moat. She looked down, where the ducks, all eight of them, bobbed along. Jealously, Miranda watched them. They didn't have to decide about printing a paper! None of them had to stand up to someone who was always standing up for what she believed in! *I wish I were a duck*, Miranda thought, walking along the path and running right into Chef Blue.

"Ooof," Chef Blue said.

"Sorry," Miranda said. "I didn't see you."

"No problem." Chef Blue sighed sadly.

But I do have a problem, Miranda thought.

"Duck," Chef Blue said. "That's waterfowl, right?"

Confused, Miranda nodded.

"I have a problem," Chef Blue said.

"Me too," Miranda said softly.

"You first," Chef Blue said.

So Miranda told Chef Blue about the *Girls Gazette* issue two. Chef Blue asked a lot of questions, like *Was the newspaper some kind of homework?*, and when Miranda said no, Miss Kinde knew nothing about it, he asked more questions, so Miranda told him about the first issue and about the *Boys Bugle*, which led to her talking about the swings being taken away, the Limburger cheese doughnut, her secret note, and rule eighty-one. All this information led to more questions, and so, as the sun dipped behind Mount Coffee, Miranda told the beginnings of the girls-versus-boys battle in 3B, which, she realized, had started with a game of tag.

"Wow," Chef Blue said when Miranda had finally finished. "That *is* a problem."

Miranda nodded. "I don't know what to do!"

"I'm sure if you put your mind to it, you'll think of a plan," Chef Blue said.

"That's the problem," Miranda said. "Maude's the planner. She was the commander and the editor in chief. Not me."

Chef Blue nodded thoughtfully before saying, "Well, as Eleanor Roosevelt said, 'You must do the thing you think you cannot do.'"

Miranda looked at the ducks. Do the thing she thought she couldn't do? What would that be? Maude had all the ideas and speeches. Maude had all the buttons!

"What's *your* problem?" she asked to be polite and to take her mind off of her own problem.

Chef Blue's problem was nearly as complicated as Miranda's. He was in a pickle about a royal dinner. Except pickles would not be on the menu, because all of the guests had a range of food allergies and dislikes.

"You see," Chef Blue said, "the Duke of Salisbury won't eat waterfowl, poultry, red meat, or anything green. Or orange."

Miranda nodded.

"And the Lady of Wiffle, who is nuts for nuts, has a terrible seafood allergy. Duchess Adelina loves fish stew but can't eat rice, nuts, sugar, wheat, pasta, potatoes, or cheese."

"Wow," Miranda said.

Chef Blue nodded miserably.

Chef Blue and Miranda looked down at the moat, where the ducks continued to float happily, free from worries of a royal dinner menu and a printing press.

And then, from the other side of the moat, nestled along the edge of the Unknown Forest, Miranda heard that strange chirping sound again.

"Do you hear that?" she asked.

Chef Blue shook his head.

"You don't?" Miranda tilted her head. "It sounds like . . . a chicken?" Her heart leapt. *Could it be?*

"Sorry, but I don't hear anything."

Miranda's heart sank. The noise had stopped, and she knew she would never figure out what to do.

27

MIRANDA TAKES A SICK DAY

The following morning, Miranda informed her parents that she wasn't going to school.

"Are you ill?" Queen Mom (also called QM) looked concerned. For someone who, not that long ago, hadn't wanted to go to school at all, Miranda had never asked for a day off. In fact, most days, Miranda went to school extra early and stayed super late.

Miranda shook her head. "I feel fine."

"Then why aren't you going to school?" KD asked.

Miranda took a deep breath. Unlike Maude, she couldn't give a speech on the spot. But in a surprising and fantastic burst of middle-of-the-night inspiration, she'd actually thought of one, wrote it down, and practiced it several times this morning. "There comes a time," she said as nobly

as she could, "when a person must do the thing they think they cannot do."

QM and KD stared at Miranda.

"What I mean," Miranda said, "is that sometimes a person must stand up for what they believe in."

QM and KD nodded.

Miranda glanced at her notes. "And sometimes, for a person to stand up for what they believe in, they have to miss school to look for a chicken in the Unknown Forest."

"A chicken?" KD asked.

"The Unknown Forest?" QM said.

"Yes. I need to stop a war."

"A war?" QM and KD asked.

Miranda nodded. "Just for today. I'll go to school tomorrow."

KD cleared his throat. "You want to skip school to look for a missing chicken, which will stop a war."

Miranda nodded.

QM and KD looked at each. Then they looked at Miranda.

"Okay," said her parents.

"You don't have to go to school today," KD said.

"But someone must go with you to look for the chicken." QM sounded stern. "You're forbidden to enter the Unknown Forest alone."

Miranda made a face, but secretly she totally agreed with that rule.

28

THE LOST AND FOUND CHICKEN

In the end, it was Chef Blue who found Rosalie. He went with Miranda into the Unknown Forest because he wanted to look for mushrooms, which he had happily realized he could serve at the royal dinner party later that evening.

"Chicken!" he hollered when he came face to face with Rosalie, who was cheerfully pecking at some pink crumbs.

Miranda ran over. "Rosalie!" she said. "I'm so glad to see you."

"It looks like she's been very well cared for," Chef Blue said, pointing to a blanket and two bowls—one with water and the other with crumbs. Miranda smelled the crumbs, and then, feeling especially brave after giving a speech and going into the Unknown Forest all in the same day, she tasted them. They were horribly sweet, but Miranda didn't even spit them out, because she now knew with 100 percent certainty who had stolen the chicken and how she could end the 3B war.

29

MIRANDA'S FIRST DELIVERY

True to her word, Miranda returned to Mountain River Valley Elementary early Wednesday morning. She found Maude sitting on top of a soccer ball, which was on top of the rusty lunchbox, reading her chicken-training book.

"You're back!" Maude exclaimed. "I was dreadfully worried. Did the boys hide your glasses? Put itching powder in your fancy shoes?"

"No," Miranda said loud and clear. "The boys had nothing to do with my absence."

"Oh." Maude sounded a little disappointed. "Where are the copies of *Girls Gazette* issue two? I can't wait to see them!"

Miranda took a deep breath. "I don't have them."

"But you're the publisher!"

Miranda held out a sparkly pink envelope. "This will explain," she said mysteriously.

30

MIRANDA'S SECOND DELIVERY

It took a while, but Miranda finally discovered Donut in the sandbox under a mountain of sand, surrounded by the little kids who used to play in the sandbox before the 3B boys took it over. When the sandbox kids saw the princess, they ran off. (Then they slowly crept back, since it was cool to see a princess so close.)

"We need to talk," Miranda said softly.

"You're the enemy," Donut said. "We cannot speak."

"But I wrote the note about the cheese." Miranda held out a sparkly pink envelope. "And I know about the chicken."

Silently, Donut pushed his left arm through the sand. Miranda handed him the envelope and then, just as quickly as she'd appeared, she was gone.

Princess Miranda Rose Lapointsetta requests the honor of your company at the castle today at four o'clock in the afternoon. There will be a chicken.

P.S.: Please use the main castle entrance.
P.P.S.: Please don't tell anyone about this.

Princess Miranda Rose Lapointsetta requests the honor of your company at the castle today at four o'clock in the afternoon. There will be doughnuts.

P.S.: Please use the main castle entrance.
P.P.S.: Please don't tell anyone about this.

31

MAUDE AND DONUT'S LONG WALK TO THE CASTLE

The rest of the day dragged for Maude and Donut, who wanted to know why Miranda had suddenly and rather formally invited each of them to the castle. But Miranda stayed silent and busy. When she wasn't taking a practice exam, she kept writing things down in Hillary's old managing editor notebook.

When the dismissal bell finally rang, Miranda told Maude that Blake, her driver, was picking her up because she needed to run a small errand. Would Maude meet her at the castle?

"Sure," Maude said. "Being alone will give me time to think about some new revenge plan for the boys."

Except a few feet from school, Maude discovered she wasn't alone.

Donut was right in front of her.

It would be just like Donut to go to the castle when he wasn't invited, Maude thought angrily.

Donut, who didn't know Maude was behind him, was thinking about doughnuts. He hoped he'd be able to eat them without thinking about cheese. He also wondered if any of them would have pink sprinkles.

When Donut got to the castle, he stopped at the ornate gate. Since he'd never been inside, he wasn't sure what to do.

But then, from out of nowhere, Maude appeared, reached her hand inside an opening in the gate, and pushed a tiny button.

Just like that, the gates opened.

Maude walked in.

Donut followed.

Maude turned around and stared at him.

Donut stared back.

"What are you doing here?" they asked at the same time.

"I'm here about a chicken," Maude said.

"Well, I'm here about some doughnuts," Donut replied.

"What?!" Maude shrieked. "Miranda wouldn't invite you! *You're* the enemy!"

"I *was* invited!" Donut held out his invitation, which had been neatly tucked into his jacket pocket.

It took Maude several minutes, but eventually she dug her crumpled invitation out of her bag.

"They say the same thing!" Donut said.

"Except for the doughnut and chicken parts," Maude said.

"Where's Miranda?" Donut asked.

Maude and Donut looked all

around the huge lawn surrounding the castle, but Miranda was nowhere.

"Look!" Donut pointed across the lawn at a long table on a patio. "I think my doughnuts are there!" He took off running.

Maude ran, too. At the exact same time, they saw an elaborate display of doughnuts, and right in the middle of the table, Rosalie was resting on a fancy chicken bed.

"Hooray!" Donut and Maude hollered.

But just as Donut reached for a doughnut and Maude reached for her chicken, Miranda

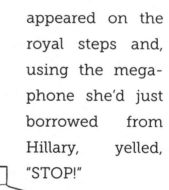 appeared on the royal steps and, using the megaphone she'd just borrowed from Hillary, yelled, "STOP!"

32

THE TRUCE

"DON'T TOUCH THAT CHICKEN, MAUDE!" Miranda hollered. "DON'T TOUCH THAT DOUGHNUT, DONUT!" Miranda walked down the long flight of stairs. When she reached the bottom, she put the megaphone on the table.

"Welcome," she said quietly. She stepped in between Maude and Donut and the table.

"Sorry I'm late!" The impartial referee with the big ears and enormous backpack panted as he sprinted across the lawn. Once he was on the patio, he rummaged through his bag and pulled out his referee shirt, the whistle, and an old-fashioned judge's wig.

"What's going on?" Maude sputtered.

"I invited the impartial

referee so there'd be two girls and two boys," Miranda said. "But mostly because he's so impartial."

The referee-judge nodded.

"But why?" Maude and Donut asked.

"We need a truce," Miranda said.

"A what?" Donut asked.

"A truce is a noun that means a stop to fighting," the referee-judge explained.

"You want a truce between me and Donut?" Maude asked.

Miranda nodded. "And between *all* the girls and boys in Three B. You're the . . ." Miranda paused to think of the right word. "Representatives!" she spit out. "This whole thing started with you two, so it should end with you two."

The referee-judge nodded.

"I don't want a truce with Donut," Maude said.

"I don't want a truce with Maude," Donut said.

"Then no chicken and no doughnuts." Miranda sounded serious.

"Miranda!" Maude gasped. "What are you doing? I thought we were best friends!"

"We are! You're the one who said actions speak louder than words. I've been trying to use my words, but it hasn't worked. So this"—Miranda put the chicken down in front of Donut and the doughnuts in front of Maude—"is my action."

Miranda took a deep breath. "And this is my speech." She glanced one last time at the managing editor notebook. "As you both know, at first, I didn't want to go to school. And there are still many things I don't like about it. School lunches. Practice exams. Music. PE. Did I say school lunches?" Donut, Maude, and the referee-judge nodded.

Miranda continued. "But once I got used to school, it turned out there were some things I *really* liked. I love Miss Kinde, of course. And the smell of newly sharpened pencils. I love swinging with Maude at recess. I like Norbert's stories and Felix's gluey creations. I loved our class play."

"*Banana Pants* forever," Maude said quietly.

Donut, who'd been a reluctant (but excellent) lead, nodded slightly.

"But Three B doesn't feel like a class anymore. I liked being a class most of all. And that's why Three B *needs* a truce. The end." Relieved that her speech was over, Miranda took a deep breath and bowed.

"That was a brilliant speech, Miranda," Maude said. "I am extremely impressed with your action *and* your words."

"Thank you," Miranda said. "And also, Maude, I won't publish the *Girls Gazette* issue two. I think you know that it's just not the kind of stuff we'd want anyone to read."

Neither Donut nor the referee-judge had any idea what Miranda was talking about, but Maude nodded.

"I put the original in the fireplace last night," Miranda said. "The burning was witnessed by royalty with a range of food allergies and diets. No one else will ever see issue two."

"Thank you," Maude said, suddenly extremely

relieved. *What had she been thinking when she wrote all those stories?* And if issue two had been printed! Maude didn't dare imagine the paper the boys would've written, and then the girls would've written another issue, and things would have gotten even worse. Miss Kinde definitely would have found out! Parents would have been called! Perhaps great fortunes would've been lost!

"Thank you," Maude said again. "And a million thanks for finding Rosalie."

Miranda looked at Donut.

"I stole your chicken!" Donut blurted out. "Because you put *cheese* in my doughnut."

"You got the swings taken away!"

"Because you stopped tag!"

"Because it was really annoying when you played it inside."

"It was?" Donut sounded surprised.

Maude nodded.

"Why didn't you tell me?" Donut asked.

"I . . ." For the first time, Maude wondered why she hadn't just told Donut to stop. "Well, you crashed into me."

"Because I didn't see you bending over your bag," Donut said. "And I said sorry."

Maude looked at Miranda. Miranda nodded. "He did. It was quiet and quick, but he did say sorry."

"Well . . . but." Maude was feeling unusually speechless. *What was happening?* And then she remembered the biggest injustice of all! "But you forbade Desdemona from playing tag! Because she's a girl."

Donut made a face.

"You said girl tag was forbidden. At last Monday's recess." Maude looked at Miranda. "You heard! Tell him."

"Well, Desdemona did say something about 'girl tag' and . . ." Miranda felt worried. *What if her big action was a terrible mistake?*

Donut looked confused. Maude looked furious. Miranda looked troubled. The impartial referee-judge looked, well, impartial. But then Donut jumped up and yelled, "Squirrel tag!"

Everyone looked at him.

"Desdemona didn't say, 'girl tag.' She said, 'squirrel tag'!" He sounded excited. "I forbade Desdemona from squirrel tag, but *not* because she's a girl."

"What's squirrel tag?" Maude asked.

"Desdemona pretends she's a squirrel. Which is fine. Squirrels are great. But when Desdemona plays squirrel tag, she just twirls around singing, 'I'm a squirrel, I'm a squirrel' a million times."

The girls looked at him.

"When she's playing squirrel tag, she just collects acorns and sings. She never tags anyone! Which is not how you play! That's why I said I won't play squirrel tag with her anymore. I'll play squirrel soccer with Desdemona and I'll play tag with Desdemona, but not squirrel tag."

Miranda looked at Maude. "That does sound like Desdemona," she said.

Maude had to agree. She looked at Miranda, at her chicken, at the impartial referee-judge, and finally at Donut. *Squirrel tag*, she thought. *How silly*. But what wasn't silly was how quickly everything had happened and how she'd forgotten the most important thing of all: Donut was her friend!

Maude took a deep breath. "I'm sorry about the cheese in your doughnut, Donut. It was a truly terrible thing to do."

Donut nodded. "I'm sorry I stole your chicken, Maude. I know how much you love her. I tried to take good care of her. Did you know she loves pink doughnut sprinkles? She'll do anything for them. But I'm sorry. About the swings and, well, everything."

"Me too."

Sorrowfully, Donut and Maude looked at each other.

"I think the Three B truce could be that there's no more *inside* tag," Miranda said excitedly. "Since that's why this whole mess started."

"I won't break that rule," Donut said eagerly.

Miranda and Donut looked at Maude. But Maude, to their surprise, hesitated. "I like a rule as much as the next person, but . . . what about if there's just no more inside tag in school or in grocery stores or operating rooms? Places like that."

Donut, Miranda, and the referee-judge stared at her.

"I'm just thinking that inside tag inside a *castle* could be fun." Maude pointed toward the enormous castle in front of them.

Donut's eyes grew wide as he looked at the castle and then at Maude. He stuck out his hand.

Maude shook it.

33

TUG-OF-WAR IS REALLY AWESOME

Early Thursday morning, Maude walked over to the girls and resigned as commander.

"You can't resign," Hillary told her. "We already fired you."

"I know," Maude said. "And it was a good move. From now on I'm only commanding myself. I'm resigning to make it extra-official."

Then she walked across the playground and over to Donut and said, "Good morning!" She was even louder than normal so that, even without Hillary's megaphone, everyone on the playground would hear her.

"Hello, Maude!" Donut boomed back.

"Want a doughnut?" She took a mound of lumpy dough out of her bag and held it out toward him. "My dad didn't use as much sugar as he should've, but they're still tasty."

Donut hesitated but then picked it up and took a bite. "Delicious," he pronounced. "How's training Rosalie with pink sprinkles?"

"Great," Maude said. "She didn't pee inside at all last night!"

Then, without much fanfare, the boy and girl representatives made it so that the girls and boys of 3B simply began doing things together again. At lunch, Maude sat with Fletcher and Felix, who both had colds, so they didn't mind the smell of her Roquefort cheese sandwich. Donut sat with Desdemona and Agatha and helped invent a new game called salamander soccer. During recess, which was inside because it was raining, Norris, Fletcher, and Hillary started working on a ten-thousand-piece puzzle of a tree in a famous forest. Saeed asked Agnes if she wanted to study comma rules, which she did.

After recess, one boy and one girl told Miss Kinde that they needed to meet with Principal Fish.

"Are you sure?" she asked.

"One million percent," Donut and Maude said.

Miss Kinde was neither sad nor confused by this. In fact, secretly, she was thrilled.

Together, Maude and Donut carried a large box into Principal Fish's office. Principal Fish stroked his long mustache while Maude and Donut confessed to faking their innocent-by-stander injuries. Once they were done, he told them that they'd broken rule number six in the

Official Rules of Mountain River Valley Elementary by lying to the principal.

"Yes," Maude and Donut said. "We know. We're sorry."

Principal Fish tugged the left side of his mustache and then the right. "PERHAPS A SUITABLE PUNISHMENT WOULD BE FOR BOTH OF YOU TO STAY AFTER SCHOOL AND ASSIST THE THREE VERY TALL MEN WITH FANCY SUITS, SUNGLASSES, AND TOOL BELTS, WHO WILL BE REINSTALLING SOME OF THE PLAYGROUND EQUIPMENT THAT HAS RECENTLY BEEN REMOVED."

Donut and Maude agreed instantly.

Early Friday morning, Principal Fish boomed the not-so-startling announcement that he'd been wrong about the dangers of tag. He went on to say that not only did tag not break rule eighty-one, but it was also a wonderful and healthy form of playground entertainment, and he actually *encouraged* the whole school to play! When it wasn't raining, he added.

Friday afternoon, when the sun returned, Miss Kinde eagerly ushered 3B out for recess. To everyone's delight, the swings and the balance beam were back. Naturally, Miranda and Maude headed for the swings, and Hillary sprinted to her beam. Deciding it was finally safe to put her soccer ball down, Desdemona kicked it as hard as she could. Agnes kicked it as hard as *she* could back. A group of 3B boys started playing tag. But then, as Saeed was leaping toward Fletcher, he spotted the long yellow rope partially buried in the sandbox.

"Tug-of-war!" Saeed hollered, holding up the rope. "Let's play tug-of-war!"

"Sure," Desdemona said. "Tug-of-war is awesome. I'll be on your team, Saeed." She kicked the soccer ball over to the sandbox kids, who finally had their sandbox back. They were thrilled, not only because they were back in their sandbox but also because they loved soccer and thought Desdemona was extremely cool.

Hillary broke rule eighty-four by doing a one-handed cartwheel on the balance beam with her eyes closed. Then she opened her eyes, jumped off the beam, and ran to Fletcher. "Victory will be mine!" she said.

"Victory will be *ours*," Fletcher corrected.

Very quickly, there were two teams. There were girls on one side. And on the other side. There were boys on one side. And on the other side, too.

"You know," Maude told Miranda, looking down at the just-about-to-start tug-of-war game from the height of her upswing, "as much as I stand by my opinion that swinging is the best part of school, that looks like it might be a lot of fun." She pointed to her classmates below.

Miranda only heard "fun," but she knew exactly what Maude was talking about. The girls jumped off their swings. Maude went to one side of the rope; Miranda went to the other.

"Where's our impartial referee-judge?" Maude jokingly asked Donut, who was in front of her.

"Right here," said the impartial referee-judge, who was standing on the rusty lunchbox with the whistle in his mouth. He was wearing the referee shirt and judge's wig.

"Wow," Donut and Maude said.

"On your marks, get set, pull!" the referee-judge hollered. He blew his whistle long and loud.

The two teams began to pull. They pulled and they tugged and they heaved and they yanked. They also grunted, groaned, laughed, and cheered. Neither team let go, and neither team crossed the chalk line, so, despite all the tugging and heaving and yanking, neither team won and neither team lost. It wasn't until the bell rang, indicating that recess was over, that they put the rope down. And then, the boys and girls of 3B cheerfully, and all together, walked back into class.

ACKNOWLEDGMENTS

Book publishing can be a battle, and I'm so grateful to have the Abrams team on my side, including Amy Vreeland, Jenn Jimenez, Siobhán Gallagher, Andrew Smith, Jody Mosley, Hana Anouk Nakamura, Mary O'Mara, Elisa Gonzalez, Mary Wowk, Nicole Schaefer, Melanie Chang, Trish O'Neill McNamara, Jenny Choy, and Brooke Shearouse. I feel so fortunate to work with Erica Finkel on another book. Erica is such a thoughtful and astute editor (or possibly a book commander) that I would follow her across any playground any day of the week.

Thanks to my agent, Rachel Orr, and a special shout-out to Oliver and Amelia, who have been rooting for Donut since book one.

I feel incredibly lucky to get to work with the magnificent Jessika von Innerebner that I still haven't had the heart to ask her to draw a horse riding a bicycle. Yet.

Thanks to Ellis Anderson, who read the first draft of this book so long ago that he might be seventeen now. Or maybe almost ten. Either way, I'll always include his birthday in my list of weekly events.

A Texas-sized thank you to my favorite family of five deep in the heart of Austin.

Love to my supportive and generous family: the extended Wunsch clan (and those who married them), the Gaffneys, and, as always, my favorite girls: Miranda and Maude. Just kidding. My favorite girls are my daughters, Georgia and Dahlia, who are generous, hilarious, and forgiving of most of my dumb jokes.

I am grateful to the children's book community of readers, teachers, librarians, reviewers, fellow writers, and booksellers who took the time to read, recommend, and promote Miranda and Maude. A special thank you to my beloved local libraries and my daughters' excellent public schools, all of which have been incredibly supportive. And finally, a fiery thank you to Mrs. Desrosiers and her Dragons! Hanover Street School's (2018–2019) 3D deserves its own book, and I can't wait for one of you to write it.

EMMA WUNSCH

Emma Wunsch likes all kinds of cheese and doughnuts but will always pass on a Limburger doughnut. One of the best parts of high school was working on the newspaper with girls and boys. *Recess Rebels* is her third chapter book in the Miranda and Maude series. She lives in Lebanon, New Hampshire, with her family.

**VISIT HER ONLINE AT
MIRANDAANDMAUDE.COM AND
EMMAWUNSCH.COM**

JESSIKA VON INNEREBNER

Jessika von Innerebner is an artist who's worked with clients including Disney, Nickelodeon, *Highlights*, and Fisher-Price. She lives in Kelowna, Canada.

**VISIT HER ONLINE AT
JESSVONI.COM**

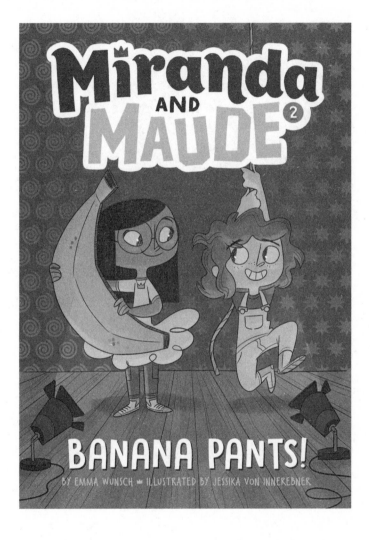

MiRanda AND MAUDE 2

BANANA PANTS!

BY EMMA WUNSCH ✎ ILLUSTRATED BY JESSIKA VON INNEREBNER

READ THESE OTHER GREAT CHAPTER BOOKS!